125 Ademor
University of Georgia
Athens, GA 30602

DOG CRAZY

Eve B. Feldman

DOG CRAZY

---

pictures by
Eric Jon Nones

Tambourine Books  *New York*

ATHENS REGIONAL LIBRARY
2025 BAXTER STREET
ATHENS, GA 30606

Text copyright © 1992 by Eve B. Feldman
Illustrations copyright © 1992 by Eric Jon Nones

All rights reserved. No part of this book may be reproduced
or utilized in any form or by any means, electronic or
mechanical, including photocopying, recording, or by any
information storage or retrieval system, without permission in
writing from the Publisher.
Inquiries should be addressed to
Tambourine Books, a division of William Morrow & Company, Inc.,
1350 Avenue of the Americas, New York, New York 10019.
Printed in the United States of America
Designed by Amy Berniker

Library of Congress Cataloging in Publication Data
Feldman, Eve.
Dog crazy/by Eve B. Feldman; pictures by Eric Jon Nones.
p. cm.
Summary: Relates Sara's humorous attempts to get a dog.
ISBN 0-688-10819-9 (rte)
[1. Dogs—Fiction.] I. Nones, Eric Jon, ill. II. Title.
PZ7F33577DO 1992 [Fic]—dc20 91-11083 CIP AC

1 3 5 7 9 10 8 6 4 2
First edition

*For my father, Zvi Sidorov, who has
always understood about girls wanting puppies,
and a whole lot more.*

E. B. F.

Contents

DOG CRAZY

1

A Problem

Sara grabbed Emily and whispered, "Don't move."

"What's wrong?" asked Emily.

"Shh," whispered Sara. "We don't want to scare that dog."

"What dog? A vicious dog? Where?"

"Not vicious! Adorable!" Sara gestured toward a lawn a few houses ahead of them. "Look at him!" She pointed to a blond cocker spaniel sniffing some bushes. "That dog doesn't live around here. I'm sure of that." Sara knew every dog in the neighborhood.

"So?" Emily asked, still trying not to move.

"So, today, April 11, 1958, will be the best day of my life!" Sara exclaimed, hugging her friend.

Emily threw her arms in the air. "What are you talking about?" she asked.

"That dog doesn't belong here. So it must be lost, right?"

"Well, maybe, but . . ."

"I'll make friends with it. And when that cute cocker spaniel follows me home, my parents will let me keep it."

Emily turned to face her friend. "I don't think your parents want a dog."

"Oh, I know that," Sara assured her. At least once a week, Sara managed to ask her parents for a dog. Every time the topic came up her parents delivered the same speech. Mr. Fine always said, "I know that you *think* you need a dog, Sara. But *I* don't think you need a dog! You don't realize how much care a dog requires. You have pets. You have fish. They need very little care yet I constantly have to remind you to feed them!"

"Fish can't play with you, Daddy!" Sara

would explain. "They can't run with you or walk with you. I can't pet a fish. Don't you see that a fish can't be a real friend?"

Then Sara's mother would answer. "Sara, you don't need a fish to be your friend. You have a sister, a brother, and many people friends!"

They just didn't understand. Sara's older sister, Rhoda, was usually too mean or too busy to be a friend and her brother Max was just a baby. Of course there was Emily. But Emily lived in her own house, a long walk away.

Sara was sure that her parents could somehow be convinced. "They don't want me to get a dog," she explained to Emily. "But if a dog got me, what could they say? They wouldn't turn away a beautiful, homeless stray that just happened to follow me home. This is just what I've been waiting for!" Slowly, Sara began to move forward. "I'm going to check that dog to make sure it doesn't have a license tag."

Emily yanked Sara back. "If that dog is a stray, it might not be safe to go near it."

"Don't worry. I'll be careful." Sara inched

forward. But before she could get close enough to see, a young man came out of the doorway. "Come on, Tango. Time to go home," the man called. The cocker spaniel bounded toward him, and they climbed into a car that had been parked in front of the house the whole time. In a flash, car, driver, and dog were gone.

Sara sat down on the curb. "Did you see that, Emily? If that dog had been lost, I could've made him follow me home." She sighed.

"It's a lucky thing you didn't," said Emily. "You could've had a police car follow you home, too, and arrest you as a dognapper!" Emily pulled Sara back to her feet. The girls walked on. "I might've been arrested as your partner in crime."

"You're right! By not getting me a dog my parents are almost driving me to a life of crime!" Sara announced as the two girls walked into Emily's house.

"How about a snack to take your mind off dogs?" Emily suggested. "My father and I baked oatmeal cookies last night."

Sara followed Emily into the kitchen. Emily's cat, Bubbles, was asleep on the window seat. Bubbles stood up and stretched. Then she jumped down and wound her way between the girls' legs. Emily scratched the cat's back. Bubbles batted Sara's shoelace between her paws.

"Maybe your parents would let you have a cat," Emily said as she set out a plate of cookies. "Cats are a lot less work than dogs, you know."

Sara chewed a cookie. *And a lot less fun*, she thought. She couldn't picture Bubbles doing any of the dog things she longed for. No fetching, no growling to scare off burglars and Rhoda, no dramatic rescues, no welcoming bark, no long walks together. Bubbles never even went outside.

"Remember how cute Bubbles was as a kitten?" Emily asked.

"Uh-huh," answered Sara. Bubbles was okay. But she'd never been a dog and never would be.

"I love my cat," said Emily. "I never think about dogs!"

"Well, you are you and I'm me!" said Sara. She tried not to sound angry but her tone gave her away. Emily picked up Bubbles and stroked her. The cat purred softly. "I guess I'd be happy with a cat, if I had a cat and a dog," Sara added thoughtfully.

"Guess that means you'd be happy with a gorilla, if you had a gorilla and a dog," said Emily.

"Fine," said Sara. "Even a tarantula and a dog." The two friends looked at each other and burst out laughing. "You know, I have a feeling that I might get a dog soon," Sara confided. "My birthday's just a couple of weeks away."

"Well, I hope you get one," said Emily. "Before we get arrested for taking someone else's. Or before you pick up a stray that bites and has rabies!"

Wishing

When Sara went home she drew a picture of the cocker spaniel that she'd almost, sort of, found and adopted. It was hard finding just the right combination of crayons to capture Tango's creamy buff color. But at last the drawing was done. "What I really need is another wall," she said aloud as she searched for a spot to hang up her drawing.

"What you really need is another head," said Sara's sister, Rhoda, from the doorway. "Then maybe you'd know it was stupid to hang dog pictures all over your room. And even stupider to talk to yourself!"

"You could knock, you know!" said Sara. "You shouldn't just sneak up on a person."

"I didn't sneak up on you. I have more important things to do than waste my time planning sneak attacks on my dog-crazy sister!"

"Just because you're older doesn't give you the right to be mean to me. I'm not mean to the baby, and I'm older than he is."

"I'm not mean to the baby, either," answered Rhoda. "Why should I be? He's cute!" She walked off.

Sara slammed the door. *Just wait until I have my dog*, she thought. He'd growl at Rhoda every time she made a nasty remark. Maybe even keep her out of Sara's room completely.

Thinking about her own dog made her feel better. She sighed. Today Tango might have been hers. But she wasn't worried. She still had more than two weeks until her birthday. Time enough for serious action.

First she'd make sure that her parents knew without a doubt exactly what she wanted for her birthday. Sara composed some poems. She put each one in an appropriate place. In her father's briefcase, she left a note on colored paper.

> *With a bark and a lick*
> *and many a trick,*
> *a dog could make*
> *your little girl happy, Pappy.*

She was proud of herself for finding such an original word to rhyme with *happy*.

Next Sara taped a poem to the fishbowl.

> *Instead of a guppy,*
> *We could have a puppy.*

She used *guppy* even though they had goldfish.

Her parents didn't say that they were convinced, but they did compliment her creative rhyming. "Pappy, huh?" laughed her mother.

Coming home from school a few days later, she found a poem hanging from her doorknob. It was in her father's handwriting.

> *We know what you wish.*
> *But have you fed the fish?*

Sara was delighted that her parents were responding. She marched straight to the fishbowl. Sprinkling fish food flakes, she watched as the two goldfish gulped down their meal.

If I had a magic wand, thought Sara, *with one poof! I could change these goldfish into dogs*. She was pretty sure that magic wands were just make-believe. And she didn't really think there was enough magic to turn goldfish into dogs. But she was sure that wishes and good luck were real. "I'll just find some good luck and figure out a way to make my wish come true!" she vowed. With only two weeks left before her birthday, some serious good luck was just what she needed.

Sara didn't tell anybody but Emily about her plan to find good luck. And she didn't think that anyone was watching when she went out in the backyard to search for a four-leaf clover. She got down on her hands and knees and started combing carefully through the lawn. She was concentrating so hard on every blade of grass that she didn't hear her sister approaching.

"Why are you crawling around on the lawn, Sara?" asked Rhoda. "Acting like the real baby you are, huh?"

"Mind your own business, Rhoda."

But Rhoda loved minding Sara's business. "I think I'll watch you. It's pretty funny. Did you lose something in the grass? Like your brains?"

Sara didn't answer.

"I've got it," said Rhoda. "You're looking for a four-leaf clover. Well, good luck, Sara! You really need good luck to find a four-leaf clover! Get it? You need good luck to find one! Ha! Ha! Ha!"

"Go away and leave me alone!" said Sara. Rhoda walked off. But Rhoda had made her so angry that she couldn't even concentrate on finding a four-leaf clover. Besides, it seemed that finding one might take forever.

I'll come up with another way to get my wish, thought Sara. That's when she remembered about eyelashes. Emily and some of the girls in school did eyelash-wishing all the time.

When an eyelash fell out, you put it on your fingertip, closed your eyes, and blew it away. If you didn't see it when you opened your eyes, your wish would come true. At least that's what Emily always said. So Sara started rubbing her eyes, trying to get some lashes to fall out. For days and days Sara rubbed her eyes. Her lashes rarely fell out even when she rubbed really hard. And it wasn't easy to rub her eyes all day without getting noticed.

"Sara, do your eyes hurt?" Mrs. Fine asked. "Maybe you need glasses."

"She's just rubbing her eyes because she's a baby," said Rhoda. "That's how babies show they need a nap."

"Oh, Rhoda," sighed Mrs. Fine, "stop teasing your sister!"

Sara tried wishing on wishbones. She told her mother, "Mommy, I love roast chicken. Can we have it more often?"

After every chicken dinner Sara asked for the wishbone. So did Rhoda. When they broke the wishbone, Sara didn't always get the bigger piece. She did get sick and tired of eating chicken.

One day, when her father was mowing the lawn, Sara asked him about wishes. "Daddy, did you ever wish for something and get what you wanted?" she asked.

"I've been wishing a lot lately," her father confessed as he mopped his brow.

"What do you want?" Sara asked eagerly.

"I'm hoping that my boss will appreciate me more. It's about time I moved ahead in the company." Mr. Fine seemed to be talking to himself as he pushed the mower harder.

Sara thought about her father's wish. She'd met Daddy's boss, Mr. Delmar, when she visited her father at work. He didn't seem to appreciate Mr. Fine, at least if remembering his children's names was a sign of paying attention to their father. "And this must be Susan," he'd said, pointing to Rhoda.

"No, that's Rhoda," Mr. Fine had corrected him. "And this is Sara," her father had explained.

Sara ran after her father. "How will you make your wish come true?" she asked him.

"Hard work is the only way I know," said Mr. Fine over the clatter of the mower.

Sara wished she could help her father. Maybe she could grow up and become one of Mr. Delmar's secretaries. They seemed to tell Mr. Delmar what to do. "You have a luncheon meeting at twelve-thirty and a two-o'clock meeting back at the office," a secretary would tell him. If Sara were Mr. Delmar's secretary, she could say, "Isn't Mr. Fine a marvelous worker, sir? How about making him your chief assistant?"

"When I grow up, I might become Mr. Delmar's secretary," Sara told Rhoda proudly.

"What a dumb idea!" said Rhoda. "I plan to be Mr. Delmar!"

"That's even dumber," said Sara. "You can't grow up to be a man!"

"No, silly, but I could grow up to be in charge of a big company like that, couldn't I?"

Sara didn't answer. She didn't want to

admit it was possible. But Rhoda was so good at being bossy that she might grow into a real boss.

Maybe her mother knew more about wishing. "Do you know how to make wishes come true?" Sara asked her.

"She's our mother, not a fairy godmother," Rhoda piped in.

"If I could make a wish come true, I'd wish that you two would stop fighting," Mrs. Fine told her daughters. Since that wasn't happening, Sara decided her mother didn't know much about wishing.

Sara even called her grandmother long-distance to ask about wishes. "I know what my mother told me," Grandma said. "Wish on a star. But make sure it's the first star in the sky, dear," explained Grandma. "And keep on trying. If you have a good wish and you keep trying, it will surely come true."

Sara had no doubt that her wish was a good one. She watched the sky when it got dark, searching for the first star. Some nights there didn't seem to be any stars. Some nights she saw too many stars. But, just in case, she always recited exactly what her grandmother had told her to say:

Star light, star bright,
first star I see tonight,
I wish I may, I wish I might,
have this wish I wish tonight.

Sara spoke in a hushed whisper. She didn't want Rhoda to hear her and spoil the whole idea, as usual. She just hoped she wasn't saying it too softly or looking at the wrong star.

As she crossed off the days on her calendar, Sara felt more and more hopeful. Just a few days left until her birthday. Her poems had given her parents clear hints about what she wanted. She'd wished every way she knew how, over and over again. Grandma could figure out what Sara was wishing for. Sara was sure about that. Why, one look at her room and anyone would know what Sara wanted more than anything else in the whole world! And if her grandmother knew how much it meant to her, maybe she could persuade her parents to say "Yes, of course the child needs a dog. The child deserves a dog. Shall we get it for her or would you like to?"

Besides, having a birthday meant that Sara was older. Older meant she could do things better—like taking care of a dog. Surely they could all see that. The more she thought about it, the more likely it seemed that her birthday would make her dream come true.

The night before her birthday, Sara rubbed her eyes, hoping for a few last minute eyelashes. She remembered to ask for help from the stars. Then she went to sleep whispering, "Maybe, maybe."

Candles,
Cake, and Canines

Sara woke up. From the minute she opened her eyes, she felt bathed in a special birthday glow. How wonderful to have a birthday, and on a Sunday too. Her party would actually be the same day as her real birthday. That was a sign of good luck. It would be a perfect dog-getting day.

She closed her eyes and tried to picture her dog. It might be a thin and sleek greyhound. It might be a big, bushy sheepdog. It might have long, floppy ears that would splash in its food. It could be a tiny fox terrier or a fancy Afghan! Even a mixed breed mutt would be fine. She laughed as she imagined a big dog with one floppy ear, one pointy ear, a square face, curly hair on one side, long hair on the other, and an Afghan's elegant tail. *Whatever it looks like*, she thought happily, *I'll love it from the minute I see it until forever.* Her mind was churning. If her parents really had gotten her a puppy, they might have hidden it in the house already.

Sara sat up in bed. She was as quiet as quiet can be. The house was quiet too. She strained to catch the sound of a puppy's soft bark or gentle breathing. But all she heard was the tick-tock of the clock by her bed.

There might be other clues, she reasoned. They'd have to buy dog food and supplies.

Still in her nightgown, Sara tiptoed into the kitchen. *This is where I'd hide dog food*, she thought. She opened every single kitchen cabinet. There wasn't even one suspicious dog food crumb. Padding around barefoot, she scanned for clues. There was nothing out of the ordinary except for assorted birthday party supplies.

At breakfast Rhoda announced, "I heard you sneaking around this morning, Sara. Bet you were trying to see if you could find what we got you for your birthday. Don't you want to guess what it is?"

Sara's mother said quickly, "Don't spoil Sara's surprise."

Baby Max gurgled in his high chair, "Ga-ga-goo-goo."

"Bet you wish Max could tell you," said Rhoda.

"I'm glad he can't," Sara replied. "I can wait to find out. Whatever it is, I am sure I'll love it." Sara looked at her mother. Mrs. Fine smiled. *Even Rhoda can't spoil my mood*, thought Sara.

By early afternoon the doorbell seemed to be one steady ring. Guests arrived, all bearing beautifully wrapped gifts. So what if none of the packages looked as if it might contain a dog? Sara didn't expect her friends to get her a dog. But maybe after she blew out the candles on the cake, her mother and father would go outside and bring in a puppy. Sara smiled. She loved imagining her dog, and she would love it even more when she saw it. Pictures flashed through her mind. What would be cuter, a Dalmatian puppy or a little basset hound? A Saint Bernard or a German shepherd? Maybe a golden cocker spaniel like the one she'd almost adopted? Would her dog have spots or be all one color? A bushy tail or a short little stub? Would it be a he or a she? Sara could barely wait to find out.

Mrs. Fine had planned a million party games, so Sara had to be patient. After what seemed like forever and a half, Mrs. Fine invited everyone to sit down at the long party table. Someone turned off the lights, and a hush fell on the room as her mother carried in the cake.

"How are you going to blow out so many candles at once?" asked her father, snapping a picture of the cake.

"No problem," said Sara. She blew them all out on the first try. "I've been practicing blowing eyelashes," she whispered to Emily.

"Tell us your wish, Sara," said Rhoda.

Sara smiled at her sister. She knew you weren't supposed to tell. "You'll see my wish when it comes true."

After the cake was finished Mr. Fine cleaned up Max's chocolate-smeared face while everyone else sat in a circle around Sara and watched as she opened her presents.

"Open this one, it's from me," said Emily.

"Ooh! I love it," said Sara when she opened Emily's box. Inside, wrapped in pale pink tissue paper, was a bright pink sweater with a furry white dog on it. Sara slipped it on over her party dress.

Mrs. Fine handed her a package. "Grandma mailed this with instructions that it be delivered to you at your party." Sara ripped off the brown mailing paper and carefully undid the dog-decorated gift wrap. Inside was a box of notepaper with pictures of dogs all around the edges. The card read, *Happy Birthday to My Youngest Special Granddaughter. May all your wishes come true! Love, Grandma.* Sara beamed.

"What great presents!" she said, and she meant it. Someone gave her dog stickers.

Rhoda gave her a white mug with a dog's picture on it. Nearly everything had a dog on it. Obviously, everyone understood how much dogs meant to her. Now Sara was even more sure that her parents must have bought her a puppy! She just knew it. She was so busy imagining her dog that it took her a few seconds to realize what her mother was saying.

"Sara, Daddy went outside to bring in your present. It was too hard to wrap, and we didn't want you to find it in the house!"

"Oh, Mommy, I love you!" said Sara. She rushed over to hug her mother. It was happening just the way she'd pictured it. Sara looked at the door. She couldn't wait to see her dog. Would her father bring it in a basket? On a leash? Wrapped in a blanket? Sara thought she'd burst from waiting.

Then the door opened and there was her father. Sara looked at him. She looked at her mother and back at her father again. Everyone in the room said, "Oh, wow! Isn't that the greatest present ever? Let me see!"

Sara couldn't believe her eyes. She didn't

know what to do. She didn't know what to say. It was a dog all right. But Sara had never seen anything like it. And she never wanted to see anything like it again! Her lips started to quiver. Her eyes began to burn. She bit her lip, determined not to cry in front of her friends.

But her friends didn't seem to notice that she was upset. They were too busy trying to get a good look at the present in her father's hands. Everyone crowded around Mr. Fine to see the dog, everyone but Sara.

"Wait a minute, folks! Make room for the birthday girl. Come here, Sara. I'll show you how it works. When your mother and I saw it, we said, 'This is just the perfect gift for Sara!' " With one hand he tried to move everyone aside. "Come on, let Sara get a good look at her birthday present," he said.

Sara looked at the dog, if you could call something that was made of wood a dog. It was a puppet, with some leather for ears and doll-like eyes. There were strings on its legs, its head, and its tail. All the strings were connected to two crossed pieces of wood. When

you moved those pieces, the wooden dog moved.

Sara watched her father demonstrate. You could make it walk. You could make it wag its tail. You could make it sit down. But you could not make it real. No one could make it real.

"What a great puppet!" said someone.

"It's so-o-o cute!" another voice called out.

Sara's friends seemed to think that it was a terrific gift. It certainly was a fancy puppet. But Sara didn't want a puppet. She'd never wished for a puppet while blowing away a zillion eyelashes. She'd never wished for a puppet while hunting through zillions of three-leaf clovers, or searching for the first and most magic star, or fighting with Rhoda over a mushy wishbone. A puppet was not what she'd asked for when she blew out her birthday candles. All she had asked for was a simple, regular, ordinary, real-live dog.

Plotting

"Let me show Sara how it works," said Rhoda.

"Not right now," said their father. "Sara seems a bit exhausted from all this excitement. She'll figure it out later." He looked at Sara. "Here, Sara. Take your dog."

Sara took the puppet.

"Thank you," she said. Her voice sounded funny. "I'll put it in my room." She took the puppet into her room and left it there, closing the door behind her. Then she walked back to her guests.

The doorbell began to ring again as parents came to pick up Sara's friends.

"Thanks, Sara."

"Happy birthday!"

"Thank you, Mr. and Mrs. Fine."

Somehow Sara remembered to thank them all, even though she felt as if she were walking around inside a bad dream. Her grandmother called just as the last guests were leaving.

"Thanks for the notepaper, Grandma," Sara said. She didn't sound very enthuasiastic.

"Are you sick or something?" her grandmother asked. "You don't sound like my cheery Sara-la."

"I'm fine, Grandma," Sara lied. Usually when Grandma called, Sara and Rhoda argued over how long they each got to talk to her, but now Sara willingly passed the phone to Rhoda.

As soon as everyone left Sara went to her room. She shut the door behind her and stared at the puppet. Then the tears that had been trying to come out, poured out. Every time she looked at the puppet she cried harder. With a sudden fling of her arm Sara threw all the stuffed animals off her bed. She curled up on top of the bedspread and sobbed. Finally she fell asleep.

The room was dark. The door creaked. Sara stirred as her mother entered the room. Silently Mrs. Fine helped Sara take off her new sweater and her good party clothes. She slipped a nightgown over her daughter's head and tucked Sara back in. Then she sat down on the edge of the bed. She put her hand on her daughter's shoulder.

"Sara, I'm sorry that you're disappointed with the dog we bought you. I really thought you were going to like it." Mrs. Fine paused. She stroked Sara's head. "Try to understand. Daddy and I don't want a real dog. This is our house too. It's a lot of work to take care of a house and three children. I'm afraid your father and I just aren't up to one more responsibility! When you grow up and have your own home, then you can have a real dog. Good night, Sara."

"Good night," Sara answered in a low voice.

When Sara woke up the next morning, the

first thing she saw was the puppet dog. *Oh, no!* she thought. *I was hoping this was all a bad dream.* "Dumb old block-of-wood dog, I wish you were real!" she muttered.

Sara sat up. *That's it!* she thought. Now she knew just what to do. This puppet was going to help her get exactly what she wanted! She bounded out of bed.

"Have a good sleep? How's your wooden woof-woof?" asked Rhoda.

Sara didn't bother answering. She just hurried about, getting washed, dressed, and ready for breakfast.

Mrs. Fine seemed surprised to see Sara happy again. "Mom, can I bring my dog to Emily's house after school?" Sara asked between bites of cereal.

"Of course, Sara," said Mrs. Fine. "I'm glad to see that you're in a better mood this morning."

After school Sara took her puppet and ran all the way to Emily's.

"Can I play with your dog?" asked Emily. "What's his name?"

"It doesn't have a name. It's just a puppet, not a puppy. I want a *real* dog. You know that. And you and this puppet are going to help me get one!"

"How can I get you a dog?" Emily wailed. "Your parents don't want a real dog. But I still think they might agree to a cat."

Sara glared at her friend. "I want a dog, not a cat or a horse or anything else!"

"*This* dog could be fun." Emily tugged at the string that made the puppet's tail wag.

"How can you say that? Don't you love your cat? Would you trade her for a cat made out of wood?"

"No way." Emily looked at Bubbles, who was arching her back nervously. "Relax, Bubbles," Emily said. She handed the puppet back to Sara and stroked her frightened pet. "I guess I see what you mean. Okay, tell me your plan."

Sara lay down on the floor next to her friend. "Well, when I woke up this morning, I looked at the puppet and wished it were alive, and then I had an idea."

"What kind of an idea?" asked Emily suspiciously.

"What if I pretend that I think this puppet is real?"

"What good would that do?" Emily asked.

"My parents will think I'm going nuts. They'll think that wanting a dog so much is making me crazy!"

Emily sat up. "And they won't be so wrong! This really is crazy." Bubbles climbed off her lap and cautiously went to investigate the puppet's strings.

"Come on, Emily. This is a perfect plan!"

Emily watched Bubbles sniff at the puppet strings and inch back cautiously. She sighed. "Do you honestly think it'll work?"

"Of course it will. I have a friend to help me make it work."

"Uh-oh. What do I have to do?" asked Emily.

"Your job is simple," explained Sara. "All you have to do is make sure that everyone notices how weird I'm acting. *I'm* the one with the hard job." Sara picked up the puppet and looked at it. "I'll have to act like this dumb puppet is real!"

"I don't see how in the world you're ever going to do that," Emily said.

"First I'll have to learn how to make this puppet move like a real dog. Come on, Emily, you can help me do that too."

"Oh, no!" shrieked Emily suddenly, as Bubbles hissed and charged at the puppet. "I think we'd better include some cat training along with puppet training."

"What did I tell you?" said Sara, calmly helping Emily untangle the strings. "This will be a cinch. Bubbles already thinks this thing is alive! Think of how convincing we'll be with practice!"

5

Acting

Every day after school Sara and Emily prac-
ticed together. They pulled the puppet strings
up and down, this way and that, trying every
possible combination. Usually Emily was the
audience, telling Sara how real the puppet
seemed. Sometimes Sara was the audience so
she could see for herself just how the wooden
dog looked when it moved. The girls helped
Bubbles get used to the puppet so that, instead
of attacking the defenseless strings, she trotted
after the moving wooden animal as if that were
her new job. After several days, the two friends

had mastered the basic movements. They could make the dog walk, sit, and even wag its tail.

"Perfect!" said Sara. "The first part of my plan is complete. Now we have to go buy some things."

"Like what?" asked Emily, following Sara out the door.

"You'll see," said Sara, leading her friend to the supermarket. With her birthday money Sara bought a leash, dog food, and a dog dish.

"Sara, you're a genius! You've thought of everything! I'm beginning to think this plan might work."

"Of course it'll work, and it's going to start tonight. Wish me luck."

That night when Mrs. Fine called "Dinner," Sara carefully walked the puppet into the dining room with her.

"Sit down, boy," said Sara as she made the dog sit. "Good boy. I'll feed you soon."

"Well, Sara, I see you know how to make your dog move. That's terrific," said Mr. Fine.

"Oh, he's very easy to train, Daddy.

Down, boy, I told you, I'll feed you soon."
Sara moved the strings and the puppet wagged
its tail.

"What did you name that thing?" asked
Rhoda.

"He is not a thing!" screamed Sara. "His
name is Woody. Come on, Woody, I'll feed
you now."

The whole family watched as Sara brought
in the dog dish and the dog food. She made the
puppet sit near the food.

Sara's mother looked at Sara's father. Sara's
father looked at Sara's mother. Sara's sister
burst out laughing.

"That is the dumbest thing I ever saw—
feeding a puppet! Wow, Sara, you really are
crazy!"

Her sister was actually helping her plan
succeed. Sara wanted to laugh. But she didn't.
She couldn't. She had to stick to her plan.

"I am not crazy. And you'd better not make
fun of me or my dog. I taught my dog to sit.
And I taught him some tricks! But I didn't
teach him not to bite. So watch out, Rhoda!"

As soon as dinner was over Sara picked up the puppet.

"Come, Woody, I'll take you for a walk. Can I go to Emily's, Mom?"

"Go right ahead, Sara," said Mrs. Fine, "but come back soon. It'll be getting dark in a couple of hours."

"Oh, Woody knows the way even in the dark," answered Sara. "But I'll come home before dark, don't worry."

As Sara walked out the door, she heard Rhoda say, "If I was Sara's mother, I *would* worry. Dogs have gone to the girl's brain, which wasn't in such great shape to start out with."

"I'll have no such talk in my home," Sara heard her father answer. "Mean jokes aren't funny!"

Sara was so happy that she wanted to run all the way to Emily's, but it was too hard to make Woody run. Besides, she thought it might help her plan if the neighbors saw her treating the puppet as if it were real. So she walked the wooden dog all the way to Emily's, even though her arms were aching by the time she got there.

Emily couldn't wait to hear all about the start of Sara's plan. Sara told her everything that had happened at dinner. She told her what her mother had said, what her father had said, and what her sister had said.

"Gee, your sister is helping you without your even asking," said Emily.

"Are you kidding? If I asked her to help she would do anything and everything to ruin my plan. No, this is perfect! Rhoda is helping me just by being her normal teasing self! See, I told you this would work. In a few days, you do your part. You come over and tell my parents that I'm acting weird. I'm sure they'll give in! This will work. It's got to!"

For the next few days Sara took good care of Woody. The weekend wasn't difficult at all. It was even fun. Max seemed to think he was watching a show. He'd sit up and clap his hands when Sara made the puppet walk around the room. Sometimes she even barked to make Max laugh.

On Sunday afternoon the whole family went to the park. Sara announced sadly that

she'd have to leave Woody home because she'd seen a No Dogs Allowed sign there.

"They didn't mean wooden dogs!" Rhoda said.

Sara ignored her sister and left Woody a bowl of water. "In case he's thirsty while we're gone," she said.

Sara's parents said nothing about the puppet. They just gave each other meaningful looks. Mr. Fine said, "Speaking of thirsty, have you fed the fish?"

The hard part started on Monday. Every morning Sara walked the puppet before school, even though it meant getting up earlier than usual. And every afternoon Sara walked the dog again. Then at night Sara put dog food in the puppet's dish and pretended to watch Woody eat it. After a while she'd clean out the dog food dish. "What he hasn't finished can be leftovers for tomorrow," she'd say out loud. And all day long she'd talk to her puppet. "Good dog, Woody. Come, Woody. Down, Woody. Sit, Woody. What a good dog!"

Every day Sara's mother looked at Sara's

father, and Sara's father looked at Sara's mother. But they didn't say anything to Sara.

Sara's sister said a lot of things. None of them were particularly nice. Sara's parents told her to leave Sara alone. Sara's baby brother helped too. He said his first word—"Dog!" Sara was thrilled! Nothing could go wrong now. The only problem was that it was taking a lot of time and energy to take care of her unreal puppet. Sara was sure that taking care of a real dog would be easier and more fun. It was hard to wake up early every morning to walk a wooden puppet. And it was hard to pretend that the wood and strings were alive. After four school days, Sara decided she'd had enough pretending. It was time to start the second part of her plan.

Sara told Emily to come over. When Emily arrived she asked Sara's mother to speak with her alone. "I think something is wrong with Sara," Emily told Mrs. Fine. "She's acting weird. She wants a real dog so much that now she seems to think that the puppet you got her is real! I thought you should know."

"Thank you, Emily," said Mrs. Fine. "You're a good friend. But we've already noticed. Sara's father and I will think about what to do."

Emily told Sara exactly what Mrs. Fine had said.

"Oh, boy," said Sara. "I told you this plan would work. You've been a big help. And you can be the first person to see my real live puppy!"

"Sara, your mom didn't say that they're going to get you a puppy," Emily said softly.

"Well, she almost said that. I know that they don't want to get me a dog. But they don't want me to be crazy. Having a dog is better than having a crazy kid. I'll keep this up just a little longer. That shouldn't be too hard."

"It would be so much easier if you'd just settle for a ca—"

"Don't finish that word, Emily!" said Sara, putting her hands over her ears. "You know what I want! They know what I want! With just a little more effort they'll give in! You'll see!"

If at First
You Don't Succeed

But it was getting harder and harder to keep pretending, especially when it poured Sunday morning. Sara lay in bed. It felt good to be snug under the covers with the rain beating down outside. There was no school, no ringing alarm clock, and no sunlight to wake her up. Sara slept until she felt someone shaking her.

"Don't you have to get up now, Sara?" It was Rhoda.

"What? Isn't it Sunday? No school. Go away. Let me sleep."

"Don't you have to walk your dog?"

"What dog?" said a half-asleep Sara.

"I don't believe my ears! Did you say 'What dog?' How could you have forgotten your wonderful wooden Woody woof-woof dog? Or have you just been pretending you think that piece of lumber is real?" Rhoda started to pull the covers off her sister. "If you have been pretending, this is the perfect day to go out and get yourself a dog, because it's raining cats and dogs out there!"

"You're not funny. And I'm not pretending. I was just sleeping and Woody is sleeping too."

"That's a good one!" said Rhoda. "How do you tell when a piece of wood is sleeping, anyway? Does it snore?"

"Oh, go away!"

"I'm just being kind to animals. Dogs have to go to the bathroom, even in the rain. So either you'll have to go outside and walk Woody in the rain, or you'll have to clean up his mess in the house." Rhoda laughed. "Actually, we both know that the only mess in this house is you and your crazy ideas! And when Mom and Dad see that you aren't walking that dumb piece of wood in the rain, they'll know you're a fake."

"Get out of my room right now, or I'll sick Woody after you!" screamed Sara.

And so it was that Sara got up and put on boots and a raincoat to walk poor Woody. She tied a plastic bag to each of Woody's feet and one to his tail. Rhoda watched and waved from the living room window.

Rhoda is a big pain, thought Sara as she came back into the house and took off her boots. But a minute later she overheard her parents talking.

"Alan," said Mrs. Fine to her husband, "did you see Sara out there in the rain? Maybe Emily's right and we really should be worried."

I knew they'd have to do something soon, Sara thought happily.

"No, dear," Mr. Fine answered. "I don't think we have to worry. Look at how sensible Sara is. I'll admit it was a bit silly to walk that puppet in the rain, but she did remember to wear a raincoat and boots! She even put plastic on the puppet's feet. Underneath this dog non-

sense Sara is a truly sensible girl. She'll get over this. All we have to do is be patient."

"I hope you're right," Mrs. Fine said. "Did I tell you that Mrs. Murphy called yesterday to tell me she'd seen Sara walking a puppet down the block?"

"So even the neighbors are enjoying the show!" Mr. Fine chuckled. "You know, maybe Sara's just doing all this to prove to us that she's capable of taking care of a dog."

"But *I'm* not capable of dealing with one more live being in this house," said Sara's mother. "Sara's still a child. Sooner or later a puppy would be my responsibility."

"Don't get so excited, Irene! We're not talking about getting a puppy!" said Mr. Fine. "The issue is whether we should be concerned about Sara's puppeteering. I'm sure there's nothing to worry about. Sara is smart and sensible. She's even beginning to remember to feed the fish!"

Sara didn't know what to think. Ordinarily she'd be glad that her father had such faith in her. But maybe he had too much faith. Smart and sensible! Ugh! Her parents might never fall for her plan. They didn't believe she was crazy. They still weren't ready to get her a dog. Sara felt like a balloon that was losing its air. It was such hard work taking care of Woody.

As Sara hung up her dripping raincoat she thought of all the effort she'd put into making *them* think that *she* thought Woody was real. She'd been so busy trying to act crazy that she hadn't had time for any of her favorite things. She hadn't read any dog books, written any dog stories, or drawn any dog pictures since her birthday. She hadn't even watched her favorite television shows, not even her most favorite show, *Queenie and Roy*. She'd missed it the day of her birthday party. She'd missed it last week, too, pretending to take care of Woody when they came home from the park.

"Well, I'm not going to miss my show to-day!" said Sara to herself. "Not if this crazy business isn't even working!"

So Sara remembered to turn on the TV when it was time for *Queenie and Roy*. She'd almost forgotten how much she loved that show. Roy was a boy and Queenie was a dog. And what a dog! Queenie was golden, brave, and smart—a perfect dog. Every week Queenie would rescue Roy or help one of Roy's friends or his family. Queenie always knew what to do.

This week Roy was baby-sitting for his two young cousins. Roy didn't notice a snake curled up in a corner of the barn. One of the cousins was moving in that direction. Sara held her breath. Would the snake attack the poor little kid? Queenie was inside Roy's house. Would *she* manage to sense the danger and save the boy?

The story was interrupted by a commercial. Sara was annoyed. She knew they'd be advertising either Ruff-Ruff dog food or Fringle's soup. She only half listened. They were talking about Fringle's. She knew all the ads by heart. A man would say how much Roy enjoyed Fringle's terrific soups. But no, that's not what the man said today! Sara jumped up. She couldn't believe her ears.

The man said that Queenie had had a litter of puppies. There was a contest. First prize was one puppy, one female puppy, one perfect Queenie puppy. It was the cutest dog that Sara had ever seen. And with Queenie for a mother it was probably the second smartest dog in the entire universe. Sara was so busy looking at the puppy that she barely heard the man's words.

"All you have to do is pick the best name for this adorable puppy! That's right, boys and girls, just send in a name for Queenie's puppy. You can enter as many times as you want, as long as every name is sent with a label from Fringle's soup. So hurry, boys and girls. Only eight days to send in your entries. All entries must be postmarked, that's mailed, by May 19. In just two weeks, the judges will pick the best name. Roy will read the name of the winner at the end of the show, two weeks from now!"

That's it! thought Sara. She could stop trying to act crazy. No more getting drenched in the rain only to hear her parents say how sensible she was! She stood up and started pacing around the room, concentrating. Her first plan, acting crazy, hadn't worked. But it had been such a brilliant idea. Anyone who could dream up that scheme would be clever enough to think of the best name for Queenie's puppy.

Sara twirled Woody around joyfully. She was sure that if she won a dog, her parents would be so proud that they'd definitely let her keep it. Sara hugged Woody and whispered in his ear, "Sensible me has found a new way!"

7

Soup and More Soup

As soon as *Queenie and Roy* was over, Sara ran
to find her mother. Mrs. Fine was just picking
Max up from his nap.

"Mommy, I am so hungry! May I have
some soup?" asked Sara.

"What kind of soup do you want?" asked
Mrs. Fine as she changed Max's diaper.

"Fringle's soup."

"Oh, Sara. I meant what *flavor* soup, not
what *brand*! Do you want pea soup, noodle
soup, chicken soup, or vegetable soup?"

"Let's see. How about noodle soup now,

chicken soup for dinner, and tomato soup for breakfast."

"Soup for breakfast? Sara, what's wrong with you now?"

Sara handed her mother a diaper pin. "Nothing's wrong with me, Mom! In fact, I've never felt better. Soup is good for you. It has vegetables and vitamins in it and uh—uh—lots of water. We learned in school that the body needs a lot of water. Some of the water in our bodies gets lost through sweat—I mean perspiration—and going to the bathroom and all. We have to put back the water we lose. Isn't that so, Mom?"

Mrs. Fine looked at Sara strangely. "Yes, the body needs water, but not necessarily soup!"

"Besides, Mom," explained Sara, "I need the labels for something."

Sara's mother made her soup. Sara took the can and carefully peeled off the label. Then she took the label back to her room and started to make a list, a list of names. Names for a female dog, names for Queenie's puppy. She thought and thought.

Princess. That's the best name, she decided. Sara took out a piece of her new notepaper. In her neatest writing, she wrote down her own name, her age, her address, and the name "Princess." Sara was sure that writing the entry on the notepaper with the little dogs on it was a perfect touch. The judges would see that this entry came from a true dog lover, a person worthy of making a good home for Queenie's puppy. Carefully and clearly, Sara wrote the contest's address on one of the envelopes. Then she sealed it, putting one of her dog stickers on the flap.

Sara searched her desk drawer and found two stamps left over from the thank you notes she'd sent for her birthday gifts. Two stamps wouldn't be enough for all her entries. Clutching her change purse, she prepared to go to the post office. Then she remembered it was Sunday. The post office would be closed.

No problem! Tomorrow after school she'd

go there and buy more stamps. She'd just have to be careful not to be seen. She didn't want anyone to know what she was up to. She didn't want to tell anyone about her new plan. Well, maybe just Emily. No, she wouldn't even tell Emily. It would be more exciting to surprise Emily too. Besides, Sara didn't want anyone else to think of a name for her pet. If she saw someone she knew in the post office, she'd pretend to be getting stamps for her mother.

The next day in school, Sara did tell Emily that her parents refused to believe she was crazy and weren't planning on saving her sanity with a dog.

"So what will you do now?" Emily asked. "Will you ask for a different kind of pet?"

Sara didn't get angry. She just smiled at her friend. "I still want a dog. I'll just have to think of a new way to get one," she said confidently.

For the next few days Sara was very busy. It was hard to think of good names. But it was even harder to eat so much soup. Sara felt as if she were drowning in soup. She was in such a hurry to eat bowl after bowl that she'd slopped soup on her new sweater. And when her homework was returned because it was covered with green pea soup splotches, Sara had to recopy every single word.

Rhoda noticed that Sara was up to something again. "Mom, why do you let Sara have so much soup?" she asked.

"Sara needs the labels for something," said their mother. "It must be something that her class is making in school. Anyway, soup is very good for you, so please leave Sara alone!"

Sara was happy that her mom was so good about the soup. She sent in many names: Princess, Goldie, Buffy, Missy, Ginger, Treasure, Emily, Gem. They were all good names. One of them would surely win.

Then, too soon, there was no more time. Sara had only one more label and one more day. "All entries must be postmarked by May 19," the announcer had said. Then the contest would be over and in a few days the judges would pick one of her names. Sara could picture exactly how it would be. Roy would say her name on television, right there on the *Queenie and Roy* show.

"Congratulations, Sara!" he'd say. Then Sara would run to tell her parents. They'd be so excited.

"We're so proud of you!" they'd say. "Of course you can keep that beautiful, wonderful puppy."

Naturally, Rhoda would insist, "I don't believe it."

But the television people would call on the telephone or send an official-looking letter or telegram, and then even Sara's sister would see that it was true. (And then Rhoda would have to say something nice, like "I'm so glad I have such a brilliant sister.")

Sara was sure it would happen just like that. The only thing she didn't know was which one of her puppy names they'd pick. Which one was best? That was a problem. If Sara didn't know which of the names was the best, how would the judges know? Sara started worrying.

I need one more name, she thought. *One terrific name so super that it's guaranteed to win.*

That was it. Sara had found the best name in the whole entire world. She was so excited that she almost screamed out loud, "I, Sara Fine, have the winning name!"

Souper—that was the magic name. It sounded just like *super*, which is what Queenie and her puppies were, but it had *soup* in it. S-o-u-p, just like Fringle's soup. Surely the judges would love that! Sara wrote down the name on her beautiful notepaper. She put the soup label in the envelope and addressed it in her neatest handwriting. She licked the stamp and carefully glued it on. Then she ran all the way to the mailbox.

"Good-bye, lucky entry," she said as the letter fluttered into the box. "Now all I have to do is wait."

Then the day finally came. Sara had slept fitfully, waking and shining her flashlight on the clock to check the time. At two A.M. she told herself she had only ten and a half hours left to wait. At four A.M. she sighed when she realized there was still a long time before the show. When daylight finally came, Sara kept

on watching the clock. The morning dragged into afternoon. Minutes had never moved so slowly before. Ten times she checked the time with her mother. Ten times she checked the time with her father.

She didn't even pay attention to Rhoda's teasing. "Forget how to tell time yourself, Sara?"

All Sara could think about was waiting for the *Queenie and Roy* show to start. She turned on the television. She sat down with Woody on her lap for good luck. There were still a few minutes left. Sara got up and paced around the room.

"Oh, Woody, soon they'll say, 'The winning name is Souper, sent to us by Sara Fine.' They will, Woody, you'll see."

The show started. For the first time in her life, Sara couldn't wait for the commercials. She barely noticed the plot. Roy's neighbor fell into a well. Roy sprained his ankle while trying to get her out. It was up to Queenie to go for help. It was exciting but not as exciting as waiting to hear her name announced, waiting to become a dog owner. And, oh, what a dog!

The first commercial showed the puppy eating Ruff-Ruff's special puppy blend dog food. "That's our Souper," Sara told Woody. The next commercial was for Fringle's, but the announcer said the name of the winner would be revealed at the end of the show. Then it was back to the story. "Enough already," Sara muttered to the television.

Finally there was Roy. He was holding the puppy, Queenie's puppy, Sara's puppy. She heard Roy's voice. "Thank you, boys and girls. You sent in so many names. The judges had a hard time. The winning name was sent in by a girl—"

"Yes, yes, I know it's me," said Sara.

"—all the way from Iowa," continued Roy.

"Iowa?" said Sara. "No, no, this isn't Iowa."

But Roy didn't hear her. He was still talking. "The winning name is She's-a-Lady."

"She's-a-Lady? That's not a name! That's

not a word! How could they not pick Souper? It must be a mistake."

But no, Roy didn't say "Sara Fine is our winner." He said another girl's name, and they called that girl right then on the telephone. Sara's telephone didn't ring. Sara didn't win. Queenie's puppy wasn't going to be Sara's dog.

Protesting

"And here's Roy giving She's-a-Lady her own name tag with her new name!" the announcer said.

"What a stupid name!" It was Rhoda's voice. She was standing in the doorway. Sara was too miserable to pay any attention to her sister. Rhoda kept on talking. "That really is dumb. Why I bet even *you* could have thought of a better name."

Sara stared at the screen, silent and sad. Rhoda never watched this show. Just Sara's luck that she was watching it now.

"And thanks again to our sponsor, Fringle's

soup, for this wonderful name-the-puppy contest," the announcer said.

"Fringle's soup, hmm," said Rhoda. "That's the soup you've been eating. Contest, hmm." She stood there with her arms folded, looking very thoughtful. "Aha! I knew you were up to something with that soup stuff. You entered that contest! What name did you send in?"

There was no point in not telling her. Even Rhoda couldn't make it any worse than it already was.

"I sent in a bunch of names. But the best one was Souper," Sara answered in a low voice. "S-o-u-p-e-r."

"I hate to tell you this, kid," said Rhoda, "but that's brilliant! Truly terrific! S-o-u-p-e-r!" There was sincere admiration in her voice. "Even *I* might not have thought of anything that clever. We must have something in common after all, little sister." Rhoda jabbed at Sara's shoulder.

Sara just sat, hugging her knees. She seemed not to notice her sister's compliments.

"Well, those judges don't know anything!"

Rhoda went on. "I'd have voted for your name, if I were a judge," Rhoda confessed.

Sara looked up. Maybe her entry *had* been wonderful. If her sister, who was almost never nice, thought it was terrific, then it probably wasn't bad at all. "So how come, do you think, I didn't win?"

"I don't know, Sara," Rhoda admitted. "Maybe you had the wrong address or forgot a stamp and it never got there."

"Uh-uh. I was super careful about the stamp and the address."

"It could have been lost, you know," Rhoda suggested. "I once saw a movie where a letter was lost for ten years."

"Maybe it did get lost," said Sara. The fact that someone else, someone who didn't even like her, had liked her name, seemed to make her feel better—better, but not good enough. She sat huddled up, resting her head against her knees.

"I'll play you one of the new board games you got for your birthday," Rhoda volunteered.

"How come?" Sara asked.

"Just because I have nothing better to do, I guess," said Rhoda. "But if you're too much of a baby to take advantage of my being nice—"

"I'll get the game," said Sara.

The girls played two rounds. Rhoda made fun of Sara only three or four times. Sara accused her sister of cheating only once. It was the best afternoon they'd had together in months.

And then Rhoda came up with an idea. "Let's get rid of the soup," she suggested.

"Huh?"

"We'll protest. No more Fringle's soup in this house. Come on." Rhoda marched into the kitchen with her sister close behind.

"We can't just throw out cans of soup," said Sara. "Mommy would get really angry."

"Who said anything about throwing it away?" said Rhoda. She began piling soup cans into a large bag. "You're not the only one around here with ideas, you know."

Sara found herself giggling when the cans

tore a hole in the bag and tumbled to the floor. Rhoda sent her to find a carton.

Before long the two sisters were outside, pulling a little red wagon full of soup. Rhoda was in charge of the wagon. Sara's job was to ring doorbells and announce, "Special soup giveaway!" Every surprised neighbor received a free can of Fringle's soup. Soon the little red wagon was empty. Rhoda scrunched herself into the wagon and made Sara give her a ride home. "After all I did for you, that's the least you can do for me," said Rhoda. Sara felt there was some truth to that. Rhoda had been surprisingly helpful.

Surprises

Rhoda's occasional niceness was the first surprise. But soon there was a bigger one.

A few weeks later Mr. Fine came home whistling. After dinner he told the girls he had some important news for them. "Looks like Sara's dream is going to come true," he said. Sara practically fainted.

"You mean you're going to get her a dog? And what do I get?" asked Rhoda.

"You get a dog too," Mr. Fine replied.

"Two dogs? We're getting two dogs?" Rhoda asked in shock. "Well, since I'm the oldest, I get to pick which—"

"What? Two dogs is the last thing this family needs!" Mr. Fine said.

"But we are getting a puppy, Daddy?" Sara was beaming.

"Not a puppy, exactly. A dog. We're getting a dog." Mr. Fine paused to look at his daughters' confused faces.

"Your father is trying to say that we are adopting his boss's dog," Mrs. Fine explained, putting Max in the playpen. "Mr. Delmar and his wife are moving to an apartment where no pets are allowed. They wanted a good home for their dog. A home with a yard."

"We're getting a hand-me-down dog?" shrieked Rhoda. "Sara, you didn't tell me that you were busy wishing for a used dog!"

"Girls! Girls!" said Mrs. Fine. "You have to understand. I would never have agreed to a puppy. A puppy needs training. A dog, a housebroken dog, is, I hope, going to be much easier."

"No problem, dear," said Mr. Fine. "This dog is five years old already, fully trained."

Rhoda turned to her sister. "Guess you won't get to use your super-souper name, after all, Sara. A used dog probably comes with a used name."

"Can't we change the dog's name?" asked Sara.

"No," said her mother. "The dog would be all confused."

Sara was slightly disappointed. Naming her own dog, training her own dog, was part of what she'd imagined as the fun of having a dog. But the chance to get a real dog was still wonderful. She pictured the dog rescuing her just like Queenie rescued Roy. "What kind of a dog is it, Daddy?" she asked.

Mr. Fine knew nothing more about the dog except that it was small. "They're bringing the dog late tomorrow afternoon," he reassured his daughters, "so it won't be long until we can see for ourselves."

A whole day seemed like a very long time to Sara and Rhoda, even though Mrs. Fine complained it wasn't enough time to get the house in order. Mrs. Fine had her daughters help dust, sweep, and vacuum. By late afternoon, Sara and Rhoda were starting to feel as overworked as Cinderella.

"Lucky Max," said Rhoda as they watched their father carry him upstairs for a nap. "He didn't do any work and now he gets to rest!"

"But he'll be sleeping when the Delmars arrive," said Sara. "And we'll be here to meet and greet my—I mean, *our* new dog."

"Actually, Sara," said Mr. Fine, "I want you and Rhoda upstairs until I call you."

"But, Daddy—" the two sisters started to object.

"No buts about it. We don't want to scare the dog with too many new faces at once," Mr. Fine told his daughters. "So stay out of sight until I call for you, please."

When the Delmars came Sara and Rhoda hid on the steps and peered through the banister. "That doesn't look like a dog," Rhoda whispered to her sister. "It looks like a hot dog. It's missing legs or something."

"Shh, it's a dachshund," Sara whispered back.

Mrs. Delmar was dabbing at her eyes with a handkerchief. "I am going to miss Sasha, aren't I, Poopsie," she crooned. She handed Mrs. Fine a typed list. "These are Sasha's favorite foods," she explained.

"I bet canned dog food is not on that list," Rhoda whispered.

Mr. Delmar carried in a small dog bed and a bag. "These are Sasha's toys," he said.

"I'm glad Sasha wasn't expecting to use the children's toys," Mrs. Fine said jokingly.

"Children?" said Mrs. Delmar.

"Girls, come downstairs and see the Delmars," Mr. Fine called. "And Sasha," he added quickly.

Rhoda and Sara came down from their hiding place on the stairs. "We have another child, a baby," Mrs. Fine was telling the Delmars.

"A baby? Oh, I do hope you won't let the baby bother my sweet little Sasha," Mrs. Delmar cautioned.

Mrs. Fine started to say something but Mr.

Fine interrupted quickly. "These are our two older children." He gestured toward Rhoda and Sara. "Both are very responsible girls. And Sara here is quite a dog fancier."

Mr. Delmar shook the girls' hands. "They do grow, children, don't they," he said. "Seems to me I've seen them at the office before, but they looked a lot younger."

Sara and Rhoda said nothing. They had both visited their father at his office and met Mr. Delmar several times. And not that long ago. But he looked much larger in their house than he did at work.

"I've never even seen the children before," Mrs. Delmar commented. She sounded worried. "Which one of you likes dogs?" she demanded.

"We both do," said Rhoda.

"I do," said Sara at the same time. Mrs. Delmar looked confused. "We both like dogs," Sara said quickly, giving her sister a *be quiet* look. "But *I'm* the one who's always wanted one."

"I do hope you're old enough to take care

of my baby Sasha," Mrs. Delmar sighed as she hugged the dog closely.

"Of course she is," Mr. Fine assured everyone, including a surprised Sara. "Besides, my wife and I are here and we're in charge." Mrs. Fine glared at him.

The conversation was interrupted by the doorbell. Mrs. Fine opened the door to admit the Delmars' driver. The children stared at the tall man with the chauffeur's cap. Rhoda yanked Sara over to peer out the window.

"Look at that limousine," Rhoda whispered to Sara. "Did you ever see anything like it on our street? The neighbors must be dying."

The driver handed the Delmars a bag and went back outside. He winked at the two sisters, who were still staring at the car.

"I'm so distraught, I almost forgot to give you this," said Mrs. Delmar as she handed the bag to Mr. Fine. "These are Sasha's collars and leashes, aren't they, Poopsie?"

"We'd better be going, dear," Mr. Delmar suggested.

"Yes, yes, of course, we must," Mrs. Delmar

replied. She kissed Sasha on the nose. "I shall miss you, Sasha Poopsie." Her voice quavered. "Here, quickly, take him, before I break down in front of your children." Mrs. Delmar thrust the dog into Mr. Fine's surprised arms. Sasha yelped once as the Delmars rushed out the front door.

Sara ran after them. "Don't worry, Mrs. Delmar," she called. "I'll take care of him. I promise." Mrs. Delmar leaned out of the car and squeezed Sara's hand gently. Then she shut the car door. As the car drove off, Sara couldn't see Mrs. Delmar's face, but she imagined the poor woman sobbing. "I promise," she shouted to the departing car. Then she ran back in to see her new dog.

Rhoda stood in the doorway and watched the Delmars drive away in their long limousine. "Wow," she said.

10

Getting Adjusted

"Not only did this dog have a great car," said Rhoda as soon as the Delmars had gone, "but he has a better wardrobe than I do." She pulled out a variety of jeweled and leather collars with leashes to match. Sasha had wriggled out of Mr. Fine's arms onto the floor. All four Fines sat on the sofa and stared at their newest family member.

"Did you hear what Mrs. Delmar called him?" asked Rhoda. "Poopsie. Do you think that's because he poops a lot?"

"Heaven forbid!" said Mrs. Fine. "Don't give him any suggestions!"

"Do something, Sara," Mr. Fine advised. "You're the dog expert around here."

Sara got up and walked toward Sasha.

"Yip, yip, yip!" the dog barked, backing away from her.

"So much for our expert," said Rhoda.

"The dog just needs time to get used to us," said Mr. Fine.

"Well, Sasha had better get used to us fast," announced Mrs. Fine. "Or back he goes, boss's dog or not. I'm not too thrilled about this idea," she added.

Sasha didn't seem too thrilled either. He ran around and around in wider and wider circles. His paws made clicking noises on the floor.

"You'd better take him out for a walk, Sara," Mrs. Fine suggested.

Sara ran after Sasha, trying to put his leash on. With the leash finally on, Sasha stopped short. In fact he refused to move. He used all his weight to cling to the ground.

"Come on, Sasha. Be a good dog," coaxed Sara. But Sasha would not budge.

"Get up, Sasha," yelled Mrs. Fine. Sasha stood up and peed on the floor. "This is crazier than Sara's puppet nonsense!" said Mrs. Fine. "That's one mess I'm not cleaning up!" She stormed out of the room.

"Don't look at me!" said Rhoda. "I'm not the one who begged for a dog." She followed her mother.

Mr. Fine and Sara cleaned up, using one of Max's diapers as a rag. "You can barely see the stain," Mr. Fine told his wife when she returned.

"I just hope you can't smell it either," said Mrs. Fine.

Just then Rhoda entered the room, holding her nose and shaking her head.

Sara grabbed her sister angrily. "It doesn't smell a bit!"

"Let go of me! First your brain stops working, then your nose!" said Rhoda smugly.

"Give the poor dog a chance," said Sara.

"Who's talking about the dog?" asked Rhoda. "I just thought it was my duty to tell you all that Max is up and made a big one."

The sound of Max crying was now audible in the background. Sasha began to howl.

"That's it, Alan. You can go get Max and clean him up," said Mrs. Fine. "I have to take Sara to the library to get information on adopting a grown dog. And don't let that dog out of your sight while I'm gone," Mrs. Fine warned her husband.

When they returned Mr. Fine proudly reported that he'd managed to get Sasha into the bathroom where the dog sat calmly and watched him bathe Max. Rhoda reported that she had called Grandma to share the day's exciting developments.

Grown dogs may be set in their ways, the library book advised. *Give them a chance to adjust to their new surroundings.* Sara tried to follow the book's advice. Within a couple of days Sasha seemed to make a bit of progress. It was just that Sasha was not what anyone expected. He agreed to be walked, if he made all decisions about when and where and how. He refused to sleep in his bed in Sara's room. He liked to sleep on top of Mr. and Mrs. Fine's bed. Mrs. Fine was not too happy about that.

Sara was eager to introduce her dog to everyone, but Sasha didn't always want to be introduced. When people came over he either hid or barked until they'd gone. Worst of all, when Emily came over he'd scamper off and vanish. He wouldn't let her pet him, not even once. Sara worried that sooner or later Emily would say something like "Too bad the Delmars didn't have a cat."

Rhoda loved Sasha. "This dog has personality!" she said. Mr. Fine loved him too, because Mr. Delmar was extremely friendly at the office. Mr. Fine was sure that having Sasha in the house would help Mr. Delmar remember the name "Alan Fine" when promotions and salaries were discussed. "I've worked hard for this company, and if he weren't so busy and absentminded, I would have had a raise a long time ago," Mr. Fine assured his wife.

Thinking about the raise helped Mrs. Fine. She didn't like sharing her bed with Sasha. But Sasha would sit outside the bedroom door and howl if they put him out of the room. It wasn't easy having baby-sitters take care of Max either. Sasha would lie down next to Max's playpen and growl at anyone who tried to pick Max up. And Sasha and Max developed a game that got on Mrs. Fine's nerves. Max would sit in his high chair and throw food on the floor. Sasha would lick up the mess. Then he'd give a little yelp. Max would clap his hands and scatter more food.

Mr. Fine said it wasn't so bad. "Max always threw food on the floor, Irene," he said reassuringly. "Now we have help cleaning it up."

But Mrs. Fine wasn't convinced. "I don't know if this is going to work out," Mrs. Fine complained to her husband on the third day. "I tried to fold laundry this afternoon. Sasha wanted to play tug-of-war with all the clean clothes! How did the Delmars survive?"

"Mrs. Delmar probably doesn't do her own laundry," Rhoda said. "Judging from Sasha's collars and that gorgeous car, the Delmars must have maids for their maids."

Sara didn't say anything. She liked Sasha, though this wasn't what she'd planned as her life with a dog. Sasha didn't seem to be much like Queenie. Sara was doubtful that she could count on Sasha to rescue her. If a ferocious lion escaped from the zoo and confronted her in the backyard, Sasha would probably run away to play with Max!

Sasha did do one wonderful thing, although Sara wasn't sure he'd meant to. On Sasha's fourth day with the Fines, a big truck pulled up to the house and Sasha started growling as a delivery man came up the walk. He was wheeling a hand wagon with a large carton.

"Does your dog bite?" the man asked nervously as Sasha growled and charged at the screen door.

"Not that we know of," Mrs. Fine said. "Take him to another room, Sara," Mrs. Fine suggested wearily. "Wait a minute, Sara. This package is for you!"

Sara stared in disbelief at the Fringle's soup

emblem on the corner of the carton. Sasha was barking at the box and trying to jump on top of it. "Calm down, Sasha," Sara said.

"Don't just stand there, Sara," said Rhoda excitedly. "This must be from that contest. Open it."

"What contest?" asked Mrs. Fine. But her daughters didn't seem to hear her.

Sara started to tear off the paper. What if the judges had changed their minds and she'd won after all? It was a big box. . . .

"It's probably a stuffed animal version of Queenie. Or a picture of Queenie, Roy, and that puppy with the dumb name. Or a picture of the puppy and the winner," Rhoda rambled on as Sara tore off the paper and screamed.

"I don't believe it! It's a case of Fringle's soup. Ick! I'll never eat a can of Fringle's soup again!" Sara kicked the carton.

"No problem!" said Rhoda. "We'll just resume Fine's soup service."

Sara smiled weakly. "As long as we get rid of it. What a stupid prize! I'm glad Sasha growled at the man!"

Mrs. Fine had trouble getting a word in. "What's this all about? Did you win a prize for eating the most soup or something?" She looked questioningly at Sara. "We're all out of soup, I discovered," Mrs. Fine said as she put Max on the floor. Max grabbed Sasha's tail. Sasha didn't even protest.

Sara handed her mother the letter that had come with the soup. Mrs. Fine read it aloud. "Dear Miss Sara Fine," it said. "Congratulations! As a finalist in our name Queenie's puppy contest, you have won a case of assorted Fringle's soup. Thanks for your participation. Hearty eating!"

Rhoda explained the contest to Mrs. Fine, who was so surprised that she barely noticed Max. Max began to crawl after Sasha. Sasha strutted after Sara. Sara marched around the room with a soup can in each hand, chanting "No more Fringle's soup. No more Fringle's soup."

Sara's parents thought that winning a case of soup was terrific. They called Grandma, who said she couldn't wait to tell all her friends

about her granddaughter, "the winner." None of them realized that as far as Sara was concerned, the only winner was the girl in Iowa with Queenie's puppy. Luckily her parents didn't object when Sara insisted on getting rid of the soup. "It would make a great donation to the charity food drive," Mrs. Fine agreed. Only Rhoda seemed to understand that Sara was deservedly angry, annoyed, downright furious at Fringle's.

Maybe Sasha understood too. Sara wondered if Sasha had known that the delivery man was bringing a package that would upset her. He'd never growled that strongly before. Was that what Queenie would have done? The carton of soup reminded her of the adorable puppy that should have been hers. At least the soup had arrived after Sara had a dog of her own. Though Sasha was not exactly what she'd been dreaming about.

It bothered Sara that Sasha didn't like cuddling, and his funny, long body was not quite the soft and furry comfort she'd expected, because he was always wriggling away on some

errand of his own. Sometimes she actually pre-
ferred playing with Woody. But she wasn't
about to complain. Even a stubborn, not-always-
friendly dog was better than no dog. She was
almost sure of that.

11

More Surprises

Barely a week after Sasha had moved in, the Delmars' limousine arrived again. This time it was unexpected and unannounced.

Rhoda was pulling into the driveway on her bike when she saw the limousine coming down the block. She ran into the house. "Mommy, they're back. The Delmars."

Mrs. Fine was frantic. "Oh, no. This house! What a mess! Help, Rhoda. Quick!" She began collecting Max's toys and dumping them into the playpen. "Where's that confounded dog anyway?"

"Sara has him in the backyard. She's still

trying to teach him to fetch a stick," Rhoda explained. "Which, if you ask me, is both useless and hopeless."

"Well, go and get her and 'Poopsie,'" Mrs. Fine ordered as she went to answer the ringing doorbell. "Why, Mrs. Delmar! What a surprise!"

"Yes, I should have called, but I just couldn't. There wasn't time and it's so . . ." Mrs. Delmar stopped as the sounds of barking and clicking feet mingled with a flash of black. Sasha had entered, dragging Sara behind him. He bounded joyfully toward his old owner. "I've missed you too, Poopsie," Mrs. Delmar cooed to the dog as she bent down and scooped him up into her arms.

"Mrs. Delmar is probably going to visit us all the time, I bet, to see 'Poopsie.' Right Mom?" Rhoda asked her mother.

"Shh, hush, oh, I hope not. I mean, I don't know," said Mrs. Fine.

"What'd you say?" Mrs. Delmar asked.

"Mom said that Sasha really missed you," Rhoda said quickly.

"Not half as much as I missed him." Mrs. Delmar rubbed her head against Sasha. "That's why I'm here."

"You can visit him anytime," suggested Sara. Mrs. Fine shot her daughter a look.

"Well, actually, this is not just a visit," said Mrs. Delmar.

Mrs. Fine sat down. She imagined that Mrs. Delmar was going to explain that her visit was actually to check up on their care and feeding of precious Poopsic.

"That's why I had to come in person. I couldn't say this over the phone." Mrs. Delmar stroked Sasha as she spoke. "I might as well just come right out and say it. I'm taking Sasha."

"For a walk?" asked Sara.

"Forever," Mrs. Delmar replied.

Mrs. Fine muttered to herself, "I knew it. She thinks we're not providing a good enough home."

"I knew you might be upset," Mrs. Delmar continued with a glance at the obviously distraught Mrs. Fine. "Sasha is so lovable. I was sure you would be instantly attached. But the truth is I just couldn't live without him!"

"Do you mean you want him back with you? Not with another family?" Mrs. Fine asked, suddenly brightening.

"Another family? Of course not. You see, I've just discovered in these past few days that Poopsie and I were not meant to be separated."

"But what about your new apartment and its rules against pets?" asked Mrs. Fine.

"We hadn't moved in yet. We'd given up our house and were staying in a hotel until the parquet tiles were installed." Mrs. Delmar sighed. "But I couldn't go through with the move. I made Lloyd, Mr. Delmar, back out of the contract." Mrs. Fine and her daughters looked confused. "We lost the down payment on the new apartment, but as I said to Lloyd, 'What's money compared to love?' " She kissed Sasha. "Don't you agree?"

Before her daughters could answer, Mrs. Fine agreed. "No doubt about it."

"We've found another place where Sasha

can be with us. We'll be a reunited family,"
Mrs. Delmar continued happily. "But of course
I realize that *you* will all be deprived and de-
pressed after having grown to love my Poopsie."
She glanced sympathetically at the Fines.

"We'll recover," said Mrs. Fine—although
Sara looked as if she might burst into tears.

"Yes, well, as I told Lloyd, 'We must make
sure the Fine family is well compensated for
their loss.' "

Sara was having trouble paying attention to
Mrs. Delmar's words. She wouldn't believe she
was about to lose the dog she had waited for so
long. Sasha may not have been the dog of her
dreams, but now there would be no dog at all.
She couldn't understand how her mother could
be looking so happy when she, Sara, was so
utterly miserable.

"So," continued Mrs. Delmar, "I've
brought you a gift." She stood up, went to the
door, and waved her hand for the driver. He
came in carrying a picnic basket. Mrs. Delmar
took the basket and handed Sasha over to the

man. "Please take Sasha outside for a few minutes," she said to the driver.

"I can take Sasha out," Sara volunteered.

"I know you can, dear," said Mrs. Delmar. "But Roger will do that now. I need you *all* here for a few minutes. I think you should see the gift I've brought." With that she put the basket on the floor and lifted one of the flaps. Out popped the head of a teeny-tiny brown version of Sasha, a little dachshund puppy.

"Ooooh," shrieked Sara as she reached out toward the tiny puppy. "He's adorable!"

"I think so too," said Mrs. Delmar. "He's from the same kennel as Sasha. Not a direct relative, mind you, but that wasn't possible."

Mrs. Fine slumped into a chair. "You needn't have done this," she said feebly.

"Oh yes, it was the least I could do," said Mrs. Delmar. "I knew that giving up Sasha could break your hearts. After all, it very nearly broke mine! So I discussed it with Lloyd, and we both decided the least we could do was get you a replacement!"

"You're wonderful!" said Sara. "So is Mr. Delmar!" She threw her arms around an astonished Mrs. Delmar. "I love him. I mean the puppy," she explained to all the confused faces. She couldn't remember ever being so happy in her whole life. "And I can even name him," she cooed.

"What about calling him Poopsie the Second?" suggested Rhoda.

"What a lovely idea!" said Mrs. Delmar. "He does have papers from the kennel and an official name." She produced an envelope from her pocket and handed it to Mrs. Fine. "But you can handle all that yourselves. I really must be going. Have to settle Sasha in and get furniture for our new place and everything." Mrs. Delmar moved to the door. "Do let me know what you call him. And I would love to watch him grow up."

"Oh yes, come and visit us anytime," said Sara warmly. Mrs. Fine gave her daughter a weak glare.

The Fines went outside to bid farewell to Sasha. "Wave bye-bye, Max," said Mrs. Fine, holding the baby up for a last view of Sasha. Sara made the puppy wave good-bye, too, as the limousine pulled away from the curb. "We'll have to keep this puppy," she announced. She snuggled the puppy close. "If we gave him away, Mom," she added, "Mrs. Delmar would never understand. Mr. Delmar might get angry. He might even fire Daddy!"

Mrs. Fine kept repeating, "I would never have agreed to a puppy. And now we have a puppy."

"But you have to adjust to an old dog's habits," Rhoda reminded her. "Sasha sure had a lot of habits. I'm going to miss him."

"Rhoda's right, Mom," said Sara. "This puppy will be trained to fit in to our household, with lots of good habits." The puppy reached up and licked her face. "He's not at all like Sasha," Sara added. "Look how he loves being petted!"

"Well, I don't know," said Mrs. Fine. "I'm too worn out to think clearly. I'll have to talk this over with your father."

Mr. Fine was overjoyed. Not by the new

puppy, but by a new promotion. Mr. Delmar had promoted him and two of his colleagues that very afternoon. "Mrs. Delmar must have been in our home while I was hearing the good news from Mr. Delmar," he said.

That news made Mrs. Fine much happier. "Maybe this isn't so bad after all," she said. "Sara got her wish. Dad got a better position with more money. Though he probably would have gotten it anyway without this dog nonsense," she sighed.

"And you got your bed back, Mommy!" added Rhoda.

Once it was decided that the puppy could stay, in fact that the puppy *must* stay, Sara called Emily. She came immediately and cooed over the friendly new dachshund. "I won't miss Sasha," she confessed. Sara understood. Sasha and Emily had never hit it off.

Rhoda and Sara phoned Grandma and took turns telling her all the details about the Delmars and the puppy.

Max seemed more interested in the picnic basket than the puppy. He sat on the floor, opening and closing the flaps. "You're going to love this puppy," Sara said. She took Max's hand and helped him gently stroke the puppy's soft brown coat.

When the flurry of phone calls was over, the business of naming and caring for the little dachshund began.

"Is there a way we could stretch his legs?" asked Rhoda. "You know, so he'd look like a regular dog."

"You must be kidding!" said Sara.

The envelope that Mrs. Delmar had left revealed that the dog's official kennel name was Hanford Winston Beaujolie III. Rhoda suggested they name him Nopoops.

"No one is going to call my dog Nopoops!" said Sara angrily.

"First of all," said Rhoda. "This is *our* dog, not your dog. And if you don't like Nopoops, we could go with my original suggestion, Poopsie the Second. Mommy will probably agree with me."

In the end, the whole family, except for baby Max, voted on the choices: Poopsie the

Second (Rhoda's idea); Super (Sara's idea—she'd show the soup company that she could use their name without the soup!); Lucky (Mrs. Fine's suggestion after discovering her husband's new salary); and Beau (Mr. Fine's suggestion). The winner was "Beau" after Mr. Fine argued that it was short for "Beaujolie," was easy enough for Baby Max to utter, and was appropriate for a short, cute dog. Sara was disappointed that her name didn't win, but her joy at having a live, lovable puppy made the name seem unimportant.

"I'd love you by any name," she whispered as she tucked the puppy into bed.

When Mr. Fine came in to kiss her good night, Sara threw her arms around his neck and gave him a big, juicy kiss. "Guess we both got our wishes after all," he said, returning her hug.

"I wonder which of my wishing methods worked," Sara said aloud.

"Maybe it was hard work, Sara, and not wishes," said Mr. Fine. "I deserve my promotion, not as a favor, but because I've been doing a good job." He looked thoughtful. "And maybe *you* earned a puppy with your hard work too," he said, looking at Woody.

After her father left the room Sara continued to wonder. Had it been wishing? If only she knew which wishing method had succeeded, she could use it again and again. Or had it been the result of hard effort? She was too happy to think clearly. She, Sara Fine, had a real-live, friendly, loving puppy. "What do you think, Woody? Was it wishing or work?" she whispered to the puppet by her bed. She had worked hard—with wishing, with Woody, with the contest, and finally with stubborn old Sasha. "I *deserve* a real-live dog," she said. "I deserve a whole houseful of dogs!"

That was it! Sara felt a surge of her old planning energy. Once her parents became used to Beau she'd make them realize what a great idea it would be to raise puppies! *Sara's Kennels!* She could picture a large sign on the front yard. She'd start by convincing Rhoda that they each needed their own dog! What a brilliant scheme! With a contented sigh Sara fell asleep, dreaming of a house full of puppies.

4/02

ATHENS REGIONAL LIBRARY SYSTEM

3 1001 00016664 6

Athens-Clarke County Library
2025 Baxter Street
Athens, GA 30606
(706) 613-3650
Member: Athens Regional Library System